The Potter Giselle

Written and Illustrated by Thomas Aarrestad

Ideals Children's Books • Nashville, Tennessee

an imprint of Hambleton-Hill Publishing, Inc.

Published by Ideals Children's Books

An imprint of Hambleton-Hill Publishing, Inc.

1501 County Hospital Road

Nashville, Tennessee 37218

800-327-5113

Printed and bound in the United States of America

ISBN 1-57102-146-9

Library of Congress Cataloging-in-Publication Data

Aarrestad, Thomas

The Potter Giselle / written and illustrated by Thomas Aarrestad.

p. cm.

Summary: King Orville the Great orders Giselle the potter to make him a magnificent pot, but his brother, King

Ludlow the Grand, insists that she make an even bigger one for him.

ISBN 1-57102-146-9 (hardcover)

[1. Kings, queens, rulers, etc—Fiction. 2. Pottery—Fiction. 3. Brothers—Fiction]

I. Title.

PZ7.A125Po   2000

[E]—dc21   98-48021

CIP

AC

To Carolyn.

—T.A.

The Potter Giselle lived in a tiny, leaning shack between two kingdoms ruled by two brother kings. Her pottery was well known in those kingdoms and far into the regions beyond.

Each pot was sturdy and every dish was light. Upon each piece was a wonderful glaze that would glow with the colors of the earth. A vase might be blue like the early morning sky, a bowl yellow-green like the first spring grass.

Giselle loved making pots. Every day she would start with a nice piece of clay. First she would knead it, and then make a ball.

She would drop it onto her wheel and, with her feet, she would spin. Then she would carefully form each pot into a one-of-a-kind creation.

After the pots were baked in the kiln she would pack them up in her cart. And hitching her
cart to her little mule, she would take them to sell in the towns.

One day she would go to the village of Wobble, in the kingdom of Orville the Great. The next day she would go to the town of Gaboo, in the kingdom of Ludlow the Grand. The pots that she could not sell in Wobble she could always sell in Gaboo.

Once, while in Wobble, she was visited by the king. He looked upon her pots with a smile.

They were bright and beautiful. They were sturdy yet light. Orville the Great knew he must have one.

Giselle was pleased and she offered the king any pot that he fancied.

But the King said, "While each of these pots is quite nice, none is grand enough for Orville the Great. What I need is a pot that's much bigger, you see, and I wish for Giselle to make it for me."

So the next day she started with a big piece of clay. First she
kneaded it, and then made a ball. She dropped it onto her
wheel and, with her feet,
began to spin.

POTTERY TODAY

Because of its size it took most of the day,
so she didn't have time to go to Gaboo.
People who looked for Giselle in
Gaboo were disappointed to find
that she had not come.
Someone claimed to have
heard that Giselle might
be making a pot for
the King of Wobble.
Later this news came
to the castle and was
heard by Ludlow the
Grand. "I must see the
pot Giselle makes for
my brother," he
said. "Perhaps I
shall have her make
one for me."

When Ludlow the Grand went to the shack of the Potter Giselle, he found Giselle just finishing the large pot she was making for Orville the Great.

"What a beautiful pot!" said Ludlow the Grand. "A treasure to behold, and I would like you to make one for me...except bigger. For a pot should be greater for Ludlow the Grand." Giselle said she would be honored to make such a pot and would start on the task the very next day.

The next morning, Giselle took an even bigger piece of clay. First she kneaded it, and then made a ball. She dropped it onto her wheel and, with her feet, began to spin.

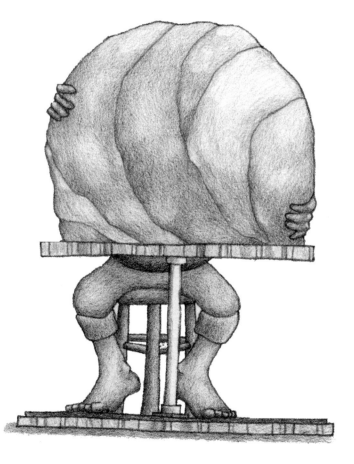

She was hard at work when a knock on her door made her stop to see who it was. It was Orville the Great, who had come to see how the work on his pot was progressing.

Giselle showed him the pot she had finished for him, but out of the corner of his eye he saw her work on the wheel.

"What is this?" the King asked.

"It's a pot," Giselle said, "that I am making for your brother...a pot to be great enough for Ludlow the Grand."

Orville, looking at this pot and forgetting his own, said, "What a beautiful pot! A treasure to behold, and I would like you to make one for me...except bigger. For while my pot is nice, it's a little too small...not grand enough for Orville the Great."

Giselle said she would be honored to make such a pot and would start the very next day.

The next morning Giselle took an even bigger piece of clay. First she kneaded it, and then made a ball. By then the ball of clay was quite big, so the carpenters were called to make her another, larger wheel. Then she dropped the ball of clay onto the wheel and, with a great deal of strength, she started to spin.

And so it went. Day after day, one King or the other would visit Giselle and admire her work with the clay. And one King or the other would ask that his pot be made just a little bit bigger.

Soon Giselle had run out of clay, so the kings sent for more from kingdoms beyond.

As the pots grew bigger, the people of Wobble and Gaboo removed Giselle's roof, then a wall, then another! Her wheels were so big that her mule had to help her spin them.

Each day one king or another would say, "A beautiful pot! A wonder to behold, but bigger, and bigger, and bigger, and bigger. More clay!"

As the pots grew still bigger Giselle needed more help. Soon, half the people from the village of Wobble were helping with the pot for their King. The same thing happened with those from Gaboo as they worked on the pot for Ludlow the Grand. Some of them helped to knead the clay, while others helped to turn the big wheels. Those who didn't work simply watched as the pots Giselle made became bigger and bigger.

The two brother kings, the Great and the Grand, argued about which pot was biggest. So did the people from Wobble and Gaboo. So that their king would win, the people worked harder and faster. Giselle could hardly keep up as the pots got bigger and the wheels still went faster, and bigger, and faster, and bigger, and faster...

... 'Til all at once there came a big BOOM and the sound of a terrible wind. Then a WHIZ and a SPLAT as the clay of the pots exploded from both wheels. All the countryside was covered with clay: the grass, the trees, the farms, the fields, and all of the people. No one could tell who was from the village of Wobble or who was from the town of Gaboo.

Then someone, maybe even one of the kings, started to laugh. Soon everyone was laughing. Giselle laughed the loudest and hardest of all.

Since no one could tell one person from the other, or even a king from a king, from then on they all lived happily together, even after they had washed themselves clean.

Then they took what was left of the two broken pots and brought them to the spot where Giselle's shack had stood. There they made the whole mess into a very nice house that any potter would be happy to have.

Here Giselle lived and worked with her clay. First she kneaded it, and then made a ball. She dropped it onto her wheel and, with her feet, began to spin. Then she would carefully form each pot into a one-of-a-kind creation, a pot that was beautiful, sturdy, and light...

...but small.